The Silence of Blackberries

Other Books by Victor Depta

Poetry

The Creek
The House
A Doorkeeper in the House
The Helen Poems

Novel

Idol & Sanctuary

The Silence of Blackberries

Victor Depta

Blair Mountain Press
P.O. Box 147
Martin, Tennessee 38237

Blair Mountain Press
P.O. Box 147
Martin, Tennessee 38237

Publisher's Cataloging-in-Publication

Depta, Victor.
The silence of blackberries / Victor Depta. -- 1st ed.
p. cm.
Preassigned LCCN 98-74248
ISBN: 0-9666608-C-3

1. Nature--Mysticism--Poetry.
2. Appalachian Region--Poetry. I. Title.

PS3554.E64S55 1999 811'54
QB198-1464

Acknowledgements

Grateful acknowledgement is made to the editors of the following publications in which these poems have appeared:

Appalachian Journal Vol. 25, No. 4 (Summer 1998) "Minor Gods in the Coal Fields"
Slant Vol. 12, (Summer 1998) "An Interest in Oneness"
Zone 3 Vol. 10, No. 2 (Fall/Winter 1996) "Pear Tree in Autumn"

Photograph by Amy Magness

Reverence for the universe is a journey
the end of which lies beyond rationality,
though many of the stretches are rational.

CONTENTS

1

A Still Beatitude

Mortise and brick and book
in a poem, is not enough
not lush
not limpid
tendrilled or rooted
ragged or rain-damp
and is not enough
lacking petals
stamens and pistil
and sweet nectar
and bees
for a still beatitude of the mind.

Interstate 40

Wildflowers
what is common in bliss
interests me
the chicory along the freeway
and other minor names I've scribbled down
on the way to Nashville--
queen anne's lace, purple clover--
where I'm to meet my daughter and her friends
downtown, for partying
and the flowers ease the tedium
for me, of the drive
yet more than that
in the calm surrounding them
the peaceableness which, once again
claims me, achingly, with the question
of the silence of blackberries
the trumpet vines and thistles
the black-eyed susans and butterfly weeds.

The Canoeing Trip

On the way to the river
while the young people chatter
clattering among their sweet flesh
sexual tensions and posturings, camaraderie and joys
I am ignored, though not unkindly so, or altogether
and I am free, thankfully
to fill the placid emptiness of what I am
as with gifts, with asters, their tall slender stems
their blossoms flung in ragtag purple along the road
and joe-pye weed, the evening primrose and partridge peas

and the estrangement, too, on the canoeing trip
the gentle blankness
the clusters of black-eyed susans along the banks
as if gypsies danced in a green shade by a green river
and wild pinks, also, and cardinal flowers
and some distance off, where the fields edge down to the water
were the richweed and the goldenrods
and then the cliffs, the water dripping from the limestone
the lichens and moss, the somber oaks and elms

and a heron
gliding across the high narrow space of blue between
        the tree lines--
its gray slender neck and breastbone
its long winged forelimbs and legs--
became the most intense of all the images
appearing in the emptiness throughout the day
because the consciousness of my state--alone, and at peace--
appearing suddenly in the sky as the heron
made me astonishingly happy.

Before the Tree Line

The ache of August
and the small irascibilities of self
are complicated by the dog days
their heavy, humid haze
though with a hint of drought in the air
and seed bearing
and yellow edging the leaves
their brown splotches and insect gnawed
and dusty
and the lobelias bloom, small, pale lavender
and the cardinal flowers, scarlet on the stalks
and salsify, pale yellow
and mallows with wide white blossoms
bindweed and trumpet vines
all these in a ditch and along a fence
a chaos of reality, the waste and profligacy of the world
the litter and trash thrown from the cars
the blur and roar and blind wind on the highway
all this before the tree line beyond which
soybeans stretch for acres
and are a relief
a simplicity for the mind.

These Perfect Days

Though the mockingbird in the great oak
sings, variable and interesting
the music is lonely as Bach's, as Mozart's
the nearly said
as if the senses spoke unintelligibly
as if the last warm autumn wind
as if the gum tree whispered with its green mouth
just below hearing, of our condition
and the pale sky, deaf and mute
gestured with its clouds
our disunion
our dear ache, blue as October

and that desire to hear
arouses in my mind the desperate thought
as I sit on the deck, attempting to hear the bird calls
to concentrate on the gum tree and the maples
and the few clouds in the sky
that the day is a sweet illusion, that behind this reprieve
these perfect days between the heat of August
and the gray slant of November, and the sleet
is an intelligence, a voice from a far-off mountain
from a distant forest saying
I am the Father of Abraham
of Rama, of Devi

and my reverie turns violent
as if holy men and priests battered at my mind
shouting down my defense
my belief that the dark voice is a lonely need
an imposition on phenomena and their infinite depth
and if the mockingbird could speak
or the gum tree or the clouds
each would say compassionately

they, child, are the illusion
their Abraham and Christ, Krishna and Shiva
all those you struggle against
are illusions

and with that, the assailants vanished
and I was free to hear, to see
that there's no fixed point
no mentality beyond phenomena
no desert mountain with its requiting deity
no avatars in the forests of India, far away
but consciousness itself
wherein one longs for union but denies the source of it
though union requires not much
a little sacrifice of the ego
and of the self's discursive thought
and with those left behind
the thoughtless consciousness can hear
fearless, in the blue sky of its dying
the joy of paradise.

The Glittering Water

If I were thorough enough with my experiences
to create a doctrine
and allow it, thereby, to give me hope of immortality
and to bring me solace in the present, and peace and joy
I would extend beyond my life the extrovertive
        mystical experience
by defining consciousness as something other than the self
as an intuitive awareness of a potential oneness
and the creative energy of the universe
as the realm of heaven

and so
when I gaze calmly at the creek
the slippery elms and birches of the tree line
the beige-bright banks
the caney water plants, the water striders and skimmers
the glittering of the sun on the rippling water
the scintillate minnows as they browse and flee
the multitudes of algae-brown sharp pebbles, the small
        black snails
the wavering ripple-shadows golden on the bed

the scene is so intensely absorbed
that I apostrophize, reaching through the creek and sunlight
crying out to their infinity which I faint into
and after awakening, I explain my consciousless experience
as paradisiacal

and so
if I were insistent about an afterlife I would say
that dying is a beatitude
and the eternal present I once awakened from
will be apotheosized eternally
at death.

The Outcrop

It is not that phenomena are less important
when the limestone
draped in ground ivy, lichen and moss
speaks *I am I am* through its surface of its infinite depth
though the names we use
magnesium carbonate and quartz
and the uses we put it to as lime and carbon dioxide and cement
deaden the voice
as we are deadened when we are put to use
made a man, a woman, our sweat and labor and pain
and cannot hear the stones speak
or hear us say *I too, I am*
because the children need, and cry

and they are not less important
though knowing that we are one
the phenomena of which we are a part become a veil sometimes
and the self becomes a veil, also
as when the threads of the wind spiders drift
and the sunlight glints on their bowed silver strings
and the undulant dun-golden dust
drifts, visible, invisible
within the shafts of sunlight through the trees

a pale fog in the rain
when the autumn afternoons enclose the trees and the self
and dawn's radiant whitening in October--
the timeless mists through which creation sweeps
brushing against the face
as the voile curtains at a boy's grandmother's house
when the child stood at the window
and the sweet spring wind swept about his shoulders
in his vanishing, long ago.

The Origins

I recall that, as a child, I once stood in a creek
bent at the waist and turning rocks to find crawfish
though way back then we called them crawdads.
I spotted one and slowly reached
with my outstretched thumb and forefinger to grab it
lifting it by its back out of the water
and studying the plated tail, tiny legs, claws, whiskers, the eyes.
Suddenly it spoke to me--

I am, I am, you are me, you are me
frightened for a moment, then speaking as a secret friend
shyly, to all that is kind in the universe
and with the matter-of-factness of infinity within itself
that small companion who appeared
surprise, surprise
and disappeared as quickly as it had shown itself

and weeds, too
even during our kids' games
cowboys & Indians, and hide & seek
when I was silent and still among the richweeds
they spoke to me, somber and deep-voiced, suddenly
we are here
and an acquiescence would overtake me
and lead with its green hands, looking back and whispering
but other voices called
yelled and shouted
I found you and you're it
you play dead, now.

Christ and the Bodhisattva

Probing my ideals for consistency
I ask why it is
I feel that the world is holy
when my reason and the fragment I know of science
says nonsense
yet my heart protests--

would a farm woman place a bushel over her dahlias
would a fledgling
featherless, turn its bulging eyes, its gaping beak away
its scrawny neck droop to its breastbone
and die
or a heifer
whose calf forced itself from her uterus
let the watery, blood-flecked creature go unsmelt
unlicked, unsuckled in the barn

and though the world devours
as an orb-weaver does the moth
as the screech owl does the mouse
the world, above its maw and gullet, its nets and claws
flourishes multiform as this blue sphere
incredible, beautiful
and blossoms as a rose
a symbol, holy and eternal, in the mind

though the mind has glimpsed the refulgent wind
the universe as unconscious
fiery and cruel beyond imagining in its plenitude
flaring about us, flame within flame in our limbs
in our hearts

and the mind, also, has turned away
beyond ego and self, which whirl like sparks in the wind
and has entered a darkness beyond flames
and seen there, serene beyond imagining
inviolable oneness

but the grieving in the world
the awareness, the Christ-need to say
let me, let me
I will bleed for you
I will hang on the thorny stem
and you can rise, blossoming beyond mouse, or moth
child, into paradise

but the sorrow in the world
where a parent, with compassionate sacrifice
sits among its children in the field
their infant tears like gems, and brimming joy
and it stretches with tenderness to the fragrant blooms
their delicate stems and leaves
and reaches to bless them
as they sigh and rest.

The Fallacy of the Absolute

When one is alone
with the ecstasy of the extrovertive mystical experience
detached, floating on the rippling, glittering creek
as a yellowed beech leaf
when one is alone
with the quiescence of the introvertive mystical experience
emptied, after the woman has left with her peck basket full
as a corn husk in the garden
there is no person, no audience, no Absolute
no One to speak to, or toward

though in the effort to communicate to others the experience
the question arises
to whom does one speak in the night
as Stevens says
To lie on one's bed in the dark, close to a face
Without eyes or mouth, that looks at one and speaks
who is that eyeless and mouthless face
not phenomena, surely
not a rose or virus
disinterestedly expanding, petals and protein

yet a face, nonetheless, one apprehends is there
not only an audience for whom ideals are blended with
phenomena for the intellect's sake
but a personage which can listen as a conscious Demiurge
as an Absolute which is concerned for the striving toward Itself
as if one rises from becoming into being
into the World Soul
and from there to the Divine Mind, the Logos
and from there into the One, the Absolute
which listens and speaks without listening or speaking
an eyeless, mouthless face

though mystical experiences do not involve a listener
but are, rather, a subject without a predicate or an object
they are without philology, grammar or syntax
isolate as a beech leaf on the glittering creek
hollow as a corn husk in the garden
whereas an act of communication presupposes listeners
          and, ultimately, the listener beyond
and thus the fallacy of the One, the Absolute.

In Boots and Denim

As though watching a sovereign city and its high spires
diminish on the horizon
the gold cross glinting in the tree line, and gone
one can, as a westerner in a wagon train
look back at the glorified loss in the east
that epoch, that ghostly kingdom gone, with an aching emptiness
and on a tableland beneath the luminous imperial sky
beneath the slivered moon and the stars in brilliant,
            startling multitudes
one can put aside the image of cottonwoods in the gulch
the hundred miles of grass, and the hearty sunflowers
and one can visualize a scene
in which a man steps behind God's throne
into the darkness and walks away
and he looks over his shoulder at the refulgent universe
where God's great throne, and Christ's, and the Holy Ghost's
are in silhouette against the blazing white cosmos
and looking forward again, he sees more darkness
and more and more
and behind the temple of Athena, more
Yahweh and Ashtaroth, more
Shiva and Parvati
and outdistancing the gods and light
he walks in a darkness until the self diminishes
to breath and heartbeat
and nothing more
and when he awakens in the morning light
he sees the cottonwoods in the gulch
the grasses for a hundred miles
and near at hand he beholds the sunflowers
dust-dry and homely in the dawn
and his breath catches, his heart quickens.

Cousin at Point Reyes

The need for hierarchy--
a golden chain to which cathedrals anchor
archbishop and priest, and children when they weep
and social discipline, guidance and harmony
by which the soul is armored
in the great host--
is most requited by theism
by a deity
by creed and doctrine and dogma
and a sweet reprieve in a bleeding chest
and pierced hands to kiss
whereas pantheism resembles a man
whose reprieve is bread, albacore and wine
whose hope is for a kiss, a bawdy bed, and sleep
and whose metaphysics begin on a strip of beach
in the surf white-flung by the wind
whose predicates spume on the rock-built jetty
in the tides and the stinging air
where hypostases soar with the gulls and pelicans
and when the apotheosis blossoms on the cliffs
as poppies and heather--blue tinged, orange-yellow--
he shouts hosannas, and sings hymns.

A Transparent Summer Morning

Urge and urge and urge,
Always the procreant urge of the world
says Whitman
whose belief is that the creative energy of the universe
is expressed sexually
I mind how once we lay such a transparent morning
and that a union of the self and the universe is mystical
a belief shared by those involved with tantric practices
with kundalini and Shakti

though Whitman's lover is rather vague
a god who is a man who is the natural world
part symbol, part sinew and bone and muscular flesh
though realistically
a mystical union occurs in isolation
a man alone, a woman alone--
therefore, Whitman's sexuality can be considered idealized
that a kelson of the creation is love
whereas the materialist's conception is otherwise
insistent chromosomes, urgent DNA
however sweet love is, the first love

though sometimes sexual copulation is so intensely pleasurable
for the man or woman who is experiencing it
that the other who is the cause loses identity
as does the experiencer's specific physicality
and so, for a time, the experiencer exists
in the contemplation of pleasure during its effects
when sexual copulation is mentally perceived as aloneness

not with a man or a woman
or the experiencer's body
but with the self in the contemplation of its own joy
and perhaps that contemplation of the intense, pleasurable self
contemplative and then ecstatic
is a method for reaching the divinity of the world
expressing itself sexually.

A Certain Kind of Intelligence

A certain kind of intelligence
dialectical, adversarial, aggressive
usually philosophical
insinuates that the mystical inclination
that a lapse of the self in union with phenomena
is an abrogation of reason
an obliteration of discriminations
uncritical, emotional, unmanly and ultimately feminine
which is sexist, of course
in that the critic personifies the mind as male
unwittingly
and phenomena as female
and that intercourse with her must be forcible
a domination of the mind
over fluid and moist and feminine reality
as if mystic love were a foregoing of something other than the ego
so I maintain
that reason is a sweaty, panting need
a yeoman naked to the waist, and muscular
laboring at his texts, preparing a field for love
and meditation is his stripping away of trousers and boots
filthy and begrimed
and contemplation is his bath in the creek
and his toweling is a beatitude
and his union is an ecstasy in the hayloft--
but such an extended metaphor as I have presented
is merely to illustrate the silliness
of philosophical sexism.

The Dandelion and the Sparrow

Formal logic requires multiplicity in order to function
and so is frustrated with the concept of oneness
like a husband whose wife refuses to quarrel
any more
and takes the child
weeping for her loss, and for her joy
and closes the door forever to his house
where he, in bitter loneliness, lives

and the child
on a rare picnic with his impoverished mother
sits pensive, idly twirling a dandelion between his fingers
and stops, and gazing at it suddenly sees and hears
I am you I am you
and startled he turns away
and goes to play as children do
as pirate and Indian and Superman

and later finds a logic more refined than his father ever pursued
which is that oneness requires multiplicity
that union cannot be achieved but by unique separateness
by the self's contemplation of the dandelion
the chipping sparrow on a twig
so fluttering quick and its instant pause
it flickering away
ah stay the glimpse of oneness
which will not stay

and as a grown-up father his kids play, and their friends
which is eternity in the delight of children
who puff their cheeks before the pale fluff of the dandelion
sending the seeds like white dreams on the wind
and boys playing Indian
and girls with their teacups and crackers on the lawn
while logic says that oneness is eternal, eternally now
as sparrows squabble and flit among the shrubs
and bees fumble on the clover.

Holiness and the Ceaseless Motion

If there is a paradox in nature mysticism
it involves the human response of holiness to a universe
whose ultimate attribute is ceaseless motion

a dilemma which can be expressed as follows:
a human being, separate from the universe
responds with holiness to it
but the ultimate attribute of the universe is ceaseless motion
therefore, the response of holiness is subjective and illogical

unless theologians and metaphysicians alter the statement
by claiming that a Being waved his hand
and as a ripple of firmament beyond His fingertips
creation stirred
or that the Unmoved Mover, the Absolute, the One
lies beyond the ceaseless motion

but we, who know, stop hoping now
though a human being must be requited somehow by the universe
because, if not, the response would languish in its illogicality
its sterility, and die

so perhaps the statement should read:
a human being responds with holiness
to the universe of which it is a part
a universe whose ultimate attribute is ceaseless motion
therefore, the response of holiness is part of the ceaseless motion

the paradox vanishes, then, in sweet humility
and holiness has a sensual origin
as when a man responds to a woman
a woman responds to a man
with adoration and a lavishing of the ideal
of worshipping with the sweetest tenderness

and thus begins the aesthetics of holiness
because, though requited and beloved
there stirs a dissatisfaction in him, in her
when caresses are not enough
and they sigh when the moon is in the pines
and when horizons streak at twilight, and at dawn

and their sweet restlessness seeps with tears
as they sigh for the unrequiting glory of the moon
and the bruised clouds of twilight, their apricot tinge, and peach
and the gold stripes of the sun, unrequiting

and then, when the aesthetic response
rises beyond despair into quietude
into awe, then holiness is near
and they become the moon, white in the pine branches
and the sun, orange and dusky in the blushed clouds
where they vanish in the ceaseless motion.

2

The Cantaloupe and Honeydew

The skin
lime smooth and roughly pink
on the two, the slick and slippery seeds
the stringy mess in the honeydew and cantaloupe
are discarded
and the swollen flesh
the scooped spoons-full of the melons
chilled in the bowl
are a feast on the tongue
and is the consequence, indescribable
of what occurs when the rind's discarded
and the seeds
for the sweet taste
the palate of nothingness
realer than the rind in the hands
realer than the slippery, sticky seeds
discarded, foregone
and the delicious scoops-full of the flesh
the pale orange, the cool lush lime
devoured, foregone
leaving the cool, damp bowl
of consciousness.

An Orange and a Rose

As though a woman sits at my table and peels an orange
she tears the textured skin from the fruit
and the pungent oil sprays on her hands
sweet, slightly acrid, the fragrance filling the kitchen.
She separates the sections
each moist and slippery, and pale orange.
She breaks the thin, translucent skin
and plucks away the seeds
and the juice of the luscious, sweet cells
wets her fingers

then she rises and walks away
disregarding the taste, as if to oppose all life
and won't caress, or ever kiss
but finds, behind her lidded eyes
that the only sanction for consciousness
is its lacking of endeavor
is its emptying of phenomenal content--
it is the only preserve against causation
the awareness of itself
a potential brilliance in darkness

and that potential she intends to realize
gaining her freedom beyond caresses, or a kiss
a world in which a rose
is not the last September blossoms along the fence
that slight affinity with the mind
that unintelligible relation
that correspondence
disinterested, often cruel, tinged with death
but an archetype out of nothingness
a symbol of dark brilliance, and bliss.

On Which Images Appear

The soul
that sweet archaic term
for consciousness, for the self
which was once contained in perspectives by da Vinci
and by Blake's Albion
by the etched hard-edge of his body
is oftentimes diffused
as in Chinese scrolls, Vermeer, van Gogh
in which consciousness is the atmosphere
the apprehending shadow and shade and light
and that atmosphere, that contemplative state
that breath, that energy
the wispy fog and golden light and glare of the sun
is the white depth on which images appear
on which phenomena, detached from their objectness
present themselves as transformations of reality
and why the matron is baptized in a golden hue
why the grain fields toss in creation's garish radiance
and why mountain crags rise out of nothingness
and why the lotus on which Buddha rests
come to be.

The White Bowl

An unremarkable man but for his misery
which in itself is undistinguished
sits at a table
and before him is a bowl of fruit
a common enough white bowl and ordinary fruit
oranges and apples, some grapes, a couple of plums
which represent desire
and conceptually he removes them as objects of phenomena
one by one, during his meditation--
something like this--
the oranges no longer exist in my consciousness
I am aware of the non-existence
the apples no longer exist in my consciousness
I am aware of the non-existence
and so on, until the bowl is empty, empty of ego
and then, with the greatest effort
he removes the bowl
which is the self
and he cannot say, then
I am aware that the self is non-existent
because there is no self
and his experience might be called the death
          of the ego
which liberates him from desire
it might be called concentration
which liberates him from the self
it might be called empty consciousness
it might be called the radiant dark
which liberates him from a union with the One
into breath and heartbeat
into oneness.

The Eternal Present

That brief hot lull--
the sky-haze and the slump of twigs
the leaves bedraggled, dusty
fatigued, even, in the wind--
drags the limbs and their ragged green
retreating through September

and the self comprehends how the ego has affected reality
how it has tilled and laid out seeds in acres
and the self observes the ego as it looks at the soybean fields
which are touched, already, with yellow
and the acres of corn
to all appearances dead, dun-brown and rustling--
the ego gazing at the actual
as it narrows through the apertures of sense
and expends itself
creating a little radiance of song
silent, sorrowful, a lament

and the self sees reality narrow its breadth
as a gorge which torments a river
whitens it violently through the narrow senses
the ego a man clinging to a rock
the torrent tearing at his limbs
to drag him down, bruised and torn
and to drown him

so on that rock
from which he will be swept into oblivion
he dreams of a past where a garden was
beside a placid, wide river glittering
and dreams of a future where his father is
and mother, and he is healed by ascension into paradise
as a wounded child

though the self considers the present
as the culmination of all past events
and all future events dependent on the present
so there is no past or present
only consciousless energy
only the eternal present
glimpsed at the moment of unity
the blinding, fainting glimpse
and the awakening into awe
into humbled reverence
into peace and sweet joy
and surrender

and the self sees the ego
high on the rock to which it has climbed
scorn the continuous divinity of the present
where the sun is a wild mustang
sweated and flecked on the plains
the foam on its mouth, on its outstretched neck
while its heart
and the surety of its hooves
is his own blood--
and the mane settles
as it bends to the grass
as it bends to drink at the ford
the chuff in its nostrils as it shakes its head
and splashes through the glittering wide river
now.

The Aesthetics of the Mystical

Without their temples
the Buddhas sit in a line like great corroded pears
and there, as weighty, termite-runneled stumps on pedestals
alongside scabrous urns, flaking Bodhisattvas
mauled temple guards and amputated dragons.
In miniature, the courtiers wander through the trefoils
chattering in plaintive fear
and on the other wall, silent as the Tao
are egrets in a branching tree.
On a screen
a prince and favored concubine, like golden carp
wend through the courtyard as the frontier guards
unclean and vacant eyed
and three months without orders
mill and argue with the clerks of court.
On another screen
are crags and the fall of a tiny stream
and near the bottom, left, a small arched bridge.
Two ornate politicians, near the center, have paused.
They spoke of the Analects, of *jen*, then were silent.
This timeless retinue
this odd and austere cousinage
these painted silks and glazes and polished wood
the bronze and jade
each halts decay around the Emperor, the Empress
who vanished like the dawn mist.

The First, High Cricket Cries

In India
where the experience of nothingness
and incorporeal consciousness is the goal
Brahman and atman
phenomena have a surplus for the senses
of many arms, lingams and yonis
breasts and buttocks, paradoxically
and ragas of the wailing self
exhausting, wearyingly beautiful

more voluptuous than our Solomon
or Christ's sweet suffering sexual flesh
or the glass rose, vast roseate near the sky
or solemn chants, hosannas or hallelujahs
of our ecstasy

and barren, then, as pines and wintry oaks
the bodiless cross, wood grain and electroplate
the plain, pale sheen
and prayers unseen without their candles
without a mother leaning to her child
and its wild cries

and God, then, unreadable as a neon sign in the sun
Christ's Only Gospel Tabernacle Church
and the awareness of immateriality
and bodiless consciousness
are sensuous, now, commonplace as September
with its crisp skies, cloudless, dry, pale blue
the asters and goldenrod in the fields
and the first, high cricket cries.

Oh Dance and Say

It is reasonable to assume that love is small
and has its place among realities inimical to it--
a man at war
the staccato and raw bursts on his chest
a wife writhing on the birth table
the breech and blood in the doctor's hands
while she is dying
and the dreariness of the day, the tedium of duty
the same and same again
and love that feigns and fails
the children wailing in the back seat
while the mother weeps at the wheel

that love is small
is reasonable among the several realities
which overwhelm it
and so our anger when the mystic nears
when he touches our sleeve and whispers
holiness is a greater love
and ranges away
serene beyond our misery, our pain, our truth
our anger at his remoteness, his dispassion
unlike dark Christ who bled
and led us to paradise

puny love
ineffectual, unreal in the context of an adversary--
the troops at the frontier, the gunnery like thunder, heat lightning
and the viruses in the blood, traitors like Sinon, like Judas--
is our reality
and the callousness of the mystic rouses our contempt
since he's not a field daisy blossoming on the battlefield
not a butterfly, sipping the salt blood on a collar
or the flies, their eggs, or the clouds
or the sky or sun, or the breeze
or the sweet acrid trembling of the weeds.

The Reprieve

With the slightest reprieve
a lapse of genocide and war
joy is irrepressible
and flits as a hummingbird
from nectarous, fluted bloom to bloom
a flicker of fleet ecstasy
a glimpse, another perhaps
and then lost

how much more, then
above all human terror, ever
it would be to spill
fountains and blossoms
and call them supernovas, dwarf stars, red giants
in pitiless joy
and delight in the maelstrom of cosmic dust, of black holes
Scylla and Charydbis
and every imagined grandeur before we fall
and blink into nothingness

and so we shrink, like Job
before the *mysterium tremendum*
and put our hands to our mouths
humbled, and less than dust
though praise the ecstasy, the plenitude in our small way
when it spumes as crepe myrtle above a fence we've built again
to dream by
and in a fountain of our own devising
to watch bright water glittering as it rises
and glittering as it falls.

Our Age Speaks Bitterly

Our age speaks bitterly
of the soul-killing Holocaust and nuclear threat
of Vietnam, of genocide in Cambodia, Bosnia, Rwanda
and our poets wound themselves
page after page
as if their themes were a sacrifice
flagellant with grief and guilt
for existence

as if to say *forgive me my little joy*
this morning
when I wanted to say
that Dawn spread out her fingertips of rose
until I saw Astyanax
his boy-body tumbling from the walls
and the homeless slump at the curb
and all the reports of death
metastasized, infectious, viral
to mortify our ecstasy

but the harmless, perhaps
the leaves of the sweet gum on the sidewalk
wined with autumn, pale red, freckled
vital with dying
perhaps they are small enough to praise without shame
to be the scattered, small, edged fans of our plenitude
and joy.

The Beech Twig and the Dragonfly

There was once a time
when joy danced in my consciousness
as though a dragonfly, stilled on a leaf
was life's bizarre delight in itself
and in the beech twig, riffling as leaf-hands on a tabla
whereby the sun, glittering on the water
was a scintillate sweet joy
was consciousness dancing
its gestures of reason at the creek bank
that ecstasy, that love
which was my unconsidered faith
and fainting into paradise

and a time, also
when the leafy twig and the dragonfly
usurped my mind with their nothing selves
their mere phenomena
and were a prelude to the greatest emptying
the loss of dance
since the benign influence reason knows
who was the rival I had vanquished from my mind
left dancing meaningless
mere chlorophyll on a twig, mere insect poised above a stream
the silence rustling, and consciousness a nothing

a time when meaninglessness claimed me
the horror of Munch's scream on a bridge
as Goya's nightmare figures about the face
as Michelangelo's damned, and Dante's
screaming and running, afire with nothingness
as dancers at an exit blocked, ablaze with horror
and wherever I turned
phenomena like the Furies screamed
dragons and Dis
and my exhausted wandering
weeping and vomiting in the weeds

until, at last
among the dewy millet and johnson grass
I heard the solace of cicadas, and the warm night breeze
and the beech tree in her pity
personified, sorrowing for me
incoherently with her green hands, her purple shadows
said to me *I am, and all of us, are the mysterium tremendum*
which you have suffered the knowledge of
and we, no more the lover and beloved, who danced there
but bruised friends, aching in our grief
spoke gently of what had been
our innocent being.

The Bottomlands

Where I've parked my truck in the dark
is silence and moonlight
and a splash then
not from a podium
or sewed and bound in a book
or from the white disks, the towers
the lumps-metal in the heavens with arcless wings
or the semi's in the distance
but a little splash among the insects' wavering chirr
and the sighing ferns and cattails
the scraping oaks and cypress
rasping and sweet-hoarse like consonants--
such a little sound, the frog-fright and splash
rings, ripples darkening in the water, the bottomlands
like vowels I seldom listen to
yet concentrate on again
in my lack of being.

The Butterfly of Ethics

Metaphysics is the butterfly of ethics
which alights and sips on the blood of soldiers the world over
who have gone hunting, sacker of cities--Troy, Moscow--
for what was once the wildebeest and bison
while the butterflies flicker from flower to inhuman flower
subtracting substance, essence, the absolute
in the candlelight of the Savior and bakhti's Krishna

meanwhile, sex is a blur of ecstasy
and the woman's groans and cries
and birth blood-flecked, yellowed, waxy
and the infant wails, gurgles and suckles
and all our truths--comforting as garish wings
as monarchs fluttering on a dung heap--flitter away
and we love the child and the cradle again

and begin again, the newborn washed and swaddling clothed
and think: do not burden the child with metaphysics
with the ontological, cosmological, teleological
or theism or pantheism or monism
but let it be, free to discover in that which nearly speaks
blossoming and devouring, honeysuckle and web
the paradox of holiness--

the confusion and illogic and despair
then come to see that suffering lies in the world of the ego
where we gather in prison yards
in markets and cattle pens where wills clash
where we kill, our eyes blood-smeared
blind to the sun while wings, illusory in their glittering
flitter about our brows

and the walking away from that
to the purples and buckeyes along the creek
to the trees and water where pain is unself-conscious
and flourishing, also, pleasure and joy without paradox
though we often grieve in the holiness there
and though we perish.

The Wedding

I went to a wedding once
at which the guests were given
not little bags of rice in tulle, tied with silver ribbons
but small plastic jars with a lid
on which was fitted a wand for blowing bubbles
and so we guests lined the sidewalk
as if blowing kisses
while the bride and groom walked beneath our well-wishes
which floated, glinting with iridescent greens and blues
above their heads
and as a medievalist would
I allegorized that each living thing
because the universe is causally dependent on it
is one with the universe and also its center
and that, since the number of living things is uncountable
among uncountable stars in galaxies like our own
the universe has an infinite number of axes
each small and vulnerable, and transparent as the air itself
which they will become, however brute or great
however undulant as glittering spheres in the sun
while the bride and groom wave and laugh
on the way to their car
which has tin cans tied to its bumper
white streamers on the aerial and doors
and on the back window
sprayed from an aerosol can of shaving cream
the ubiquitous message.

An Interest in Oneness

To my young friends I joke about mysticism
and they, relieved, kid around, also, with the subject
asking where's my crystal
will I levitate drinking beer
can I smoke during meditation
because the subject frightens them a little--
what if I got weird
what if I grew a beard to my chest
hair to my shoulder blades
and went to the Naropa Institute in Boulder
what if I abandoned them
what if I abandoned all they have affection for--
the elderly chitchat gossipy man who loves to party
who is paternal with them
whose grumpy old-man voice calls out
hey, boy, get your drunken ass in the car and let's go
and then apologizes
who calls his daughter *honey and darling*
and does the same to her young women friends--
would I forsake who they are
would I, in effect, consider them irrelevant
and die away from them
in my consuming interest
in oneness
and I, also, am a little frightened.

The Sixtieth Spring

What an old truck I have
a hundred thousand miles
the dashboard bleached, sun-split
the windshield cracked, the seat torn
the oil gauge dead, and the hazard warning switch
the headlight knob broken off--
and a draft of wind from the window
brushes past my face
so sweet that heaven itself has a fragrance
faint with paradise
while the gravel road, the sodden grass on the margin
and the barbed wire fence
disappear
and I panic like the gibbon that missed the branch
and wake, white knuckles on the steering wheel
to find myself, staring at a huge round bale of hay.

A Shawl of the Sun

What is it but loneliness brought me to the creekbank
and the nothingness I am without affection
without a hand to hold
and I have come back from there and think to myself--
after your journey, what story do you have to tell
what did you see or hear
what to say to your daughter and your friends about dignity
about self, about desire
about unrequitedness like galls on the cedar limbs
those oozing, brown-orange lumps and putrid slime
in your misery, your unhappiness when your child is distant
more than a thousand miles
when duty is thin and devotion's assumed
I know you think of me
rather than a hug, and nearby to fix dinner for

you drive to the creek, and wade, and drink some wine
wanting to wail in desolation for what's left behind
but you don't
you settle, instead, on the bank
as would an old man, a shawl of the sun about his shoulders
selecting from the rags sprung up about
a bright weed
merely to dote on, to be fond of
and find in it such a long way back
infinitely back almost, it seems, what you were
when memory fades and eternity flares for a moment
through the weed, the scraggly sweet flag, into what you are
what you more greatly were
when you were stilled on the bank
in an ecstasy by the glittering stream
and are, though in your loneliness you had forgotten--
and that is what I have to tell my daughter and my friends
what I've come back for, to explain.

3

The Minuscule of Joy

The violets, tiny things
compared to the fence they blossom along
the bank they're scattered on
their littlest blue mouths
and the wild strawberries are a half-inch full
at least, of buttery o's in the grass
their little gasps
and brilliant with surprise
comparable to the self
that sweetened minuscule of joy
as small as a two inch sun in April
where the robins leap, and mockingbirds
wing-flung and flittering in the spring
similar to the self--
mind-cloud and drift
until the ego tugs, a cage and tedium again
and then, shadows past, the latch-lift and flee
the self's small joy all free again
in the pure cloud-puffy blue
above the cedars.

A Simple Chore

With an ordinary thought
the mind leaps beyond it and says
I know, and I still am
and runs on
hurtling to one reality after another
but there is a thought
beyond which unexpectedly
the field ends
and one falls

suddenly, with a very quiet violence
though briefly, till one recovers
and miraculously
one does not wail, or weep
because of the abyss
the darkness between the washed cup
and the dish.

One stands as without implements
with nothing to alter, to trim and fit
and what little that could be done
sustaining as foundation posts, as joists and floor
the common days and years
lost now
all lost in blackness

yet one recovers
one concentrates to hold being in the mind
staring out the window
blind to the tulips and the phlox
or down at one's hands
on what so much depends

staring, to all appearances stilled beyond use
at a fine point, at the self
tinier yet, and yet
almost infinitely small.

In Its Own Kingdom

If sparrows can warp the world into a nest
and bees give birth within an octagon
why, then, shouldn't the self have a rest

from continual emptiness? Oughtn't it put on
a fluff and cellophane, cheep and buzz,
eat worms and nectar in its own kingdom?

When out of the hive, what dazzling does
the bee behold! the nectarous golds and blues
the powdery scarlets, the chaste white poses

to be possessed, and in possessing blest
with love's rough tenderness inward and out.
And when with novice wings dressed

proudly dun, the sparrow flouts
the air, what scares, what silly solemn joys
to flit in leafy heaven all about!

And when the sun, in waning, then destroys
in grief-ful fires the fields and silent trees
the haggard bee, bedraggled sparrow--envoy

and refugee among a freight of seed
sent trundling around the sun--must suffer
and the self go naked, shivering in the snow.

A Mockingbird in April

If a mockingbird were to sing
I would hear it, ringing in its throat, alone
without any need
to find a word that said, in its bright sadness
what the self is--
not the shrub, the bridal wreath
where the bird has paused with its wealthy throat
its lithe wings

its flitting in a multitude of petals
smaller than snowflakes, which fall--
the self as silent as the sprays they fell from
and silent on the lawn
when the bird has flown
the self is not that--
that lovely and petal-strewn

or the bright feathers of the bird
briefly white as it flutters to the pear tree
then hid as it sings
and then bright again, as it flings itself, raucously
to the fence
and in a gray flounce to the cedars--
the self is not that
and needs no word or summary in the calm
of its separateness.

By the Side of the Road

And all the profligate waste of the world
which neither nourishes in spring
nor stores in granaries
now blossoms, great splotches of the sun

groundsels and mustard
across the fields in swaths
and fleabane, like fleet clouds
wisps in the cumulus of the sky

flourishes by the roadside
here where the mid-south with its broomsage
its sad requiem
bends to the moist wind

of the inevitable spring
while the buttercups, gap-petaled and waxy
stiff almost as plastic, hardly stir
close to the ground as they are

where I've stopped, vaguely restless
anticipatory, with nothing to do
my truck parked by the road
but watch the geese and herons in the marshy ponds

and the swift clouds
out of the west
horizon to horizon
in the April sky.

April Poem

I have seen everything that is done under the sun;
and behold, all is vanity and a striving after wind.

You would have thought the yard
being discarded as she was
empty eyed, in rags and wailing
withered in her glory

all those months ago
would scorn the youth
striding from the south
from his Mardi gras

his Carnivals of feathered smiles
of the bronzed sheen on the breasts and limbs--
that beast who lavished on them
his lust, that callow, inconstant, roughshod blond

from the north
who abandoned his love
and left her weeping in my yard
in October--

that she would now
like a forgetful fool
bedeck herself in plum blossoms
in pear and peach

in violets and wild strawberry blossoms
spring beauties and gaudy tulips
like the trollop she is
heedless of me

who listened patiently
as she moaned through January, bitter as the wind
and pulled cold comfort about herself
disdainful as cloaks of snow

should now undrape
should powder herself with clouds, and rouge with petals
and rouse the robins and the mockingbirds--
should bare her breasts

and prance like an idiot in my yard
that she should scorn me
her dutiful suzerainty, her bodyguard
for a silly blond boy--

well, it's beyond bearing, I tell you
and I'll lower the blinds.
I'll close the drapes
and read Ecclesiastes.

The Hawkweed

It's startling to think that Keats
a hundred and seventy-eight years ago
referred to Olympus' faded hierarchy
while I, in a teasing playful mood
attend to the hawkweed
and pretend to speak as to a friend
of all things delicate
and flatter the hairy, long-stemmed
raggedy small blossoms
dull yellow, posing I suppose
as coy maiden aunts to the black-eyed susans
when a tiny tangle-petaled bloom
cried out *I am I am*
and I was ashamed to have teased so
to have caused such pain to a homely dignity
whose eternity was revealed
and I was chastened
and silent.

Her Turtles, Her Possums

I held the playthings in my hand.
They were made by my sister's little girl.
The child had come chattering
We'll make some turtles and some possums
as she held up pebbles and pecans
toothpicks, glue and paintbrushes to make everything real.

You are third removed, little niece, from the ideal
I whispered to myself as we painted and pasted.
I asked if they behaved, those friends who made her circle round
not like the odd mysterious languor of the real one
or the fat waddle of the other.

It wouldn't matter to happiness if we were twelfth removed
if I'd become the scholar I'd thought to be
or she made arks which floated among the family
except that I wasn't happy.

I had, like her, created an animal
a ferret, a white truth whose zeal frightened me
as it darted among the books which I disdained
though I wouldn't, with such violence, have disclaimed them
if I weren't plagued by a metaphysical disease.

But a child knows nothing of all that
and how could I lack all pity when she said
Now I lay me down to sleep.
I think of the sacred story
the model by which the serpent crawls
from its God's monolithic design
coiling and hissing in the rational mind.

Near the WPA Bridge

The small limbs of a water birch
like airy delicate green fans, like gestures of benediction
swag over the creek
and the creek itself, calf-deep
clear and babbling with its sweet white noise
is little
and the minnows, too
and the blue azures, and the coppers
all small
and the sunlight dappled
leaf-dallied with
as a girl does, flittering and flirting with a boy--
the scene, not more than a few yards
gazed at as if by eyes of the dragonfly
suddenly flares, blinds with its brilliance
and the mind faints
awakening as the ribs break open in wounds of joy
outpouring rapture resembling blood
and cries
and birth like dying
though the bodily form
encasing the awareness of infinitude
is silent, is motionless
and passersby on the bridge would see, merely
a man sitting on the creek bank
and not the astonishment at the martyring ecstasy
the blissful sacrifice of the self
or the blinding brilliance in the small branches of the birch
in the little creek and babbling and tiny butterflies
in the green heron paused on the other bank
and its languorous flight
and the distant trill of a cowbird
off in a field.

Minor Gods in the Coal Fields

At play on the ridges
they lap the dewdrops from the moss
and weave into fronds the ferns they've plucked, for fans
and the green snakes and the striped
lie across their napes, and the hollows of their throats
very cool, and about their wrists, like bracelets.
They feast on oak galls
the amber of pine and fungi resembling tongues
and gulp down bloodroot, its red juice

and feed the mantis tidbits of wandering wasps and wild bees
and at the outcrop, sprawl on the sandstone rubble
trailing their fingers in the sunken spring, freckled with leaf-fall
to stroke the salamanders' skin
to dip their hickory shells and splash themselves, and bathe.
They watch the ground ivy wilt, the trilliums fade
and never speak, or descend, but to entice the children.

The boys fly when they whisper to their gaping selves
out of the houses, past the slate, the coal car drops, the tipple
to lie in the milkweed pods
wide as wings on the stalks, as silken beds.
The asters pale, and pokeberries shrivel
while dreams are being ripened in these thin-boned boys.
Copperheads linger, and dragonflies hang over the pool
where the water drips from the driftmouth
        of the abandoned mine.
Sycamore bark is flaking, the scrub pines droop, mullein dies.
Heat wavers over the weedy mine road. The leaves strangle.

And the minor gods, who had descended from the ridge
who paused at the graveyard on the hill
with its flowered mounds and sockets in the grass
to mince on lichens on the stones
have found them, high in the beechnut tree
picking away the hulls at a little feast
and in bawd summary, hand in hand
the gods surround them in thrall, and in the heat of August
dance and withdraw.

The Comfort of Infinity

The idea of an endless universe eternally present
and of self-consciousness as contingent and variably intense
is disturbing
because we apprehend origins and ends
not infinitude, not past and future efflorescing now
and because self-consciousness is understood as the referent
        beyond which nothing else is
so we devise our comings into the world
our firmaments above and those below
and our essence as an origin from far away, and resembling a sun

and though self-consciousness discriminates
selecting among phenomena to make abstractions of them
considering itself a bodily object and a series of thought
it has incipiently an essence
since, by concentrating, it can expunge events and entities
and efface itself as a bodily object and a series of thought--
it can encounter its existence independent of occurrences
of inimical causation, and know itself as a reality
perpetually being, limitlessly existing, and free

but the universe won't be put aside
since in the deepest consciousness, even in the furthest ecstasy
the sea of the body washes against its shore--
however expansive consciousness is
the cosmos abides in its breath and heartbeat
and so self-consciousness, returning to itself, is humbled

is meditative as it looks outward
losing itself, experiencing an illimitable empyrean through
        a twig of the water birch
recognizing, now, infinitudes of living entities
on which the cosmos is utterly dependent
spreading everywhere about them
since they are the center, as all things equally are
and are not disturbed.

Southern Labor

All ease work, now, sweet tedious
leaves lawn rake, awkward sew
scrape woodwork, sand, wipe clean and paint
and small order in the attic--
a greasy bolt under the fan belt
hard to reach
warped miter, finger bruise
and sweeping the basement--
and balmy, door screen
a why-glad in the feathered west-pink, streaked lavender
moon-silver and Venus--the why delight
porch lingering and mow-scent night
Canaan cloudless, stars pale
and winsome words, unused to me, unsuited
the night and sweet sigh
the sorrow ease and breathing in Beulah.

The Appalachian Journey

She has so many children to love
mother has, as the earthly hen
and I am one of her brood
her blond chick, the same different
son love but similar, as goldenrod and moon
but father
he was the blank gold
the swollen forget me, the sex, the god swell
the farewell, the blond and sweet-sweat of the sun
which I had not become
and he was lost to me
ghost-god, gone from my heart
gone from perception
which was pure then
and the moon pared to a sliver
ah, pained afterthought, and gone
and the earth, also, dear blue sphere, also gone
no longer anthropomorphous, or myth, none of them
or Father or the One or the Absolute
and not the ego, that ravening will
not overwrought as the ego was
this swaying freedom, now, and the sweet self
over the roads.

Pear Tree in Autumn

To experience peace in the autumn ease
though death-charged as the pears on the lawn
the scattered splurge--wan, oval flecks--
yellowed beneath the tree
fragments of the sun's caress
his freckled roughened hands
and the sighing blue
seated so near to frost, has paused
washed clean as azure linen, as her apron
though nothing stops
in the morning or otherwise
not the pears' blotched shriveling
or the fluttering leaf-brown
or the memory of what before
was white, petals and petal-fluttering
and was green nubs and riper yet
swelling among the leaves
though all is peace, eased now as if sighing
the sweet self
lingering without disquiet
well past dawn.

September Evening

To say good-bye in the twilight
to the passions, the sweet even the pain
the paring down, the whittled slivers till all summer ends
in the hand, in the blade-sharp knife
as discursive reason
and the ineffable in the other
which I let fall
both of them
and have the moon only left to look at
and Venus, and a few faint stars
which are not tainted with symbolism
the feathered pink-gray wings of clouds
like a tinged eternity
but September, only that
when with darling-sharp, sweet notes
the mockingbirds put day to rest in a last fling
in a fluttering hymn
above the intellect and intuition
which had been bought and sold in the summer days
in the violence of storms and sweaty sun
till what is left, costless
is a song.

October Afternoon

Perhaps the frayed-fringe of the goldenrod
is enough, and the asters
airy enough in the windless beige-blue
tiny enough in the thick light, the yellowed afternoon
sifting through branches and drooping leaves
for all that is minor in death--
and is enough
since from the weeds
the brown encasements
seeds were flung like pebbles
leaving their chaff and fluff
and their rings in eternity--
enough to signify
as filaments, drift-whirled, unravelings
the small self
and to say *I know, I know*
in the slanted gold-array.

The Sweetgum

Not the *Tennessean*
the headlines or CNN
or Lear or Gloucester at the lectern
or McDonald's chattering

but the self
and the o sigh of the whitening sun
silent as the sweetgum
as the spiked seed balls on the lawn

earth brown, and the pain-bliss
reasonless as the sorrow for a scarlet
and flecked grief
while raking leaves

that luxury of the self
that vowel o and u
breeze-flickering
pale blue and cirrus

wisp and fleece-frayed
silent as lamentations
vermilion-freckled in the sweetgum
and the whitening sun.

Doves in November

This mystic love
am I to wipe it off like tears on a child's face
and walk among dry thistles
the blackberry vines and broomstraw
the burrs and sticktights
as a bitter paramour
and with cold reason watch the winter come
knowing the vaporous disk for what it is, now
the sun near solstice, and not the exhaustion of desire
and consider my love an infatuation
a teenage crush, foolish, unreasoning
that hangs like an empty milkweed pod by the fence
and the brittle grass
the hoar frost, the rabbit frost
as the disillusionments of a kid
whose mother in her green gown, and his father's gold
have gone
regents in a bark of time
leaving him to weep among gray stalks
the brown leaves curled against them
like the hands of the dead--
I am not childish, however
tear-blind, aggrieved beyond reason
but have considered the seeds
which willy-nilly scatter themselves
some smaller than grains of sand
such as the millet
and some gargantuan as the osage
some clever and clinging
and in my rambling I have startled the doves
and the panic of wings frightens me for a moment
and I see the storm coming out of the west
the louring, gray-white clouds
and turn for home
a grown man, an adult who will vanish
in time, into his entirety.

When the Chlorophyll Withdraws

The chlorophyll withdraws
as if the equinox were winged, hopelessly gaudy
trailing its ragged scarlets and foils of gold
like fires across the hills--
one watches
as would a peasant when the high, gilded coaches pass
who glimpsed the empress, curtained at her window
in gold and lace as she glanced, indifferent
at the highway--
and the leaves, like ashes, tumble in the wind
a ghostly rustling as one walks across the lawn
and store fronts burgeon with bales of hay
corn stalks and pumpkins
and children with their plastic pails and awkward costumes
shy as October phantoms, fidget at the door--
when one withdraws, interior and silent
while the days mist over, gray, and with sleet and ice storms
and days brilliant-white, and bluing white, and shadowing
and the afternoons, when snow swirls through the cedars
it is then one pauses at the window by the Christmas tree
attesting to the gentlest hope of persons everywhere in the west
that the world will last--
it is that time when one withdraws to the kitchen
and sitting at the table
one turns to the Christmas cactus
a little desert plant, seemingly without stems
its small, flat, succulent, heart-shaped leaves
each rising out of the other
and arcing to the red blossoms at the tips--
it is then one meditates on such small living things.